Rusty Red

The Sound of R

By Cynthia Klingel and Robert B. Noyed

The Child's World®, Inc.

I take my rusty red
wagon everywhere
with me.

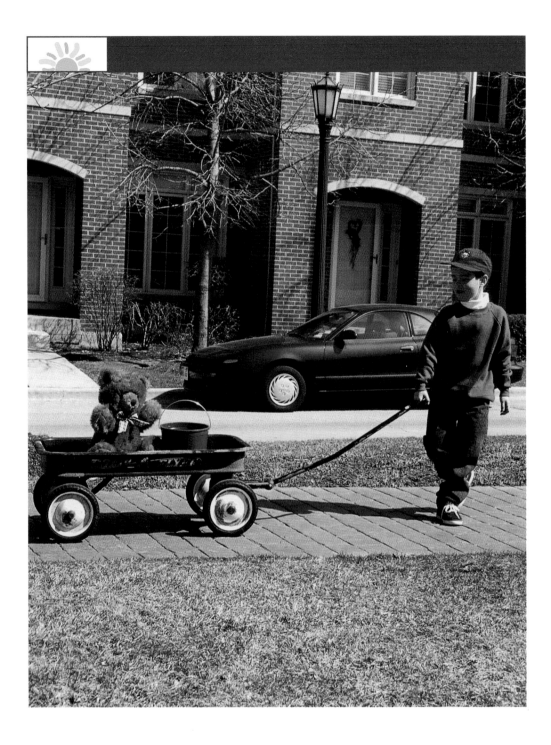

My teddy bear rides in my rusty red wagon.

I run with my rusty
red wagon.

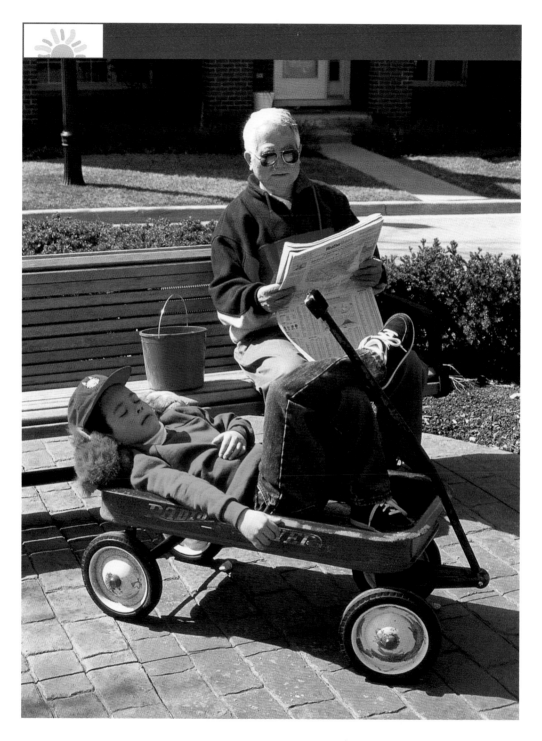

I rest in my rusty
red wagon.

I put rocks in my rusty red wagon.

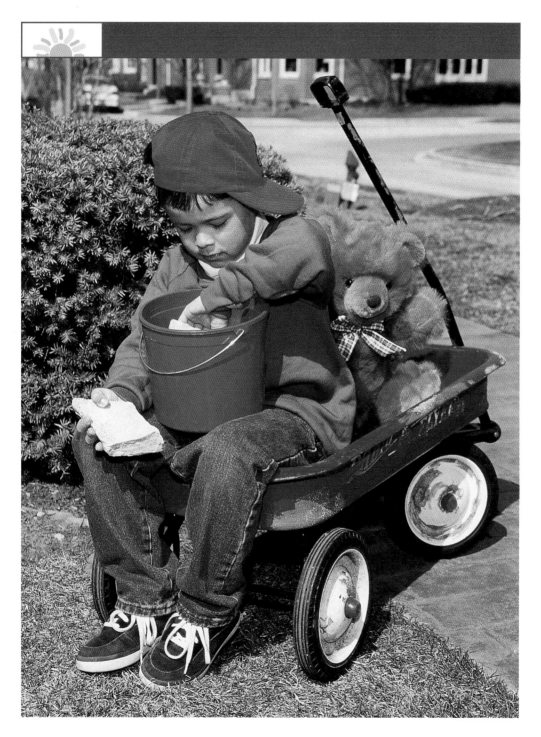

I sit on the rim of my rusty red wagon.

My grandpa rubs the
rust off my wagon.

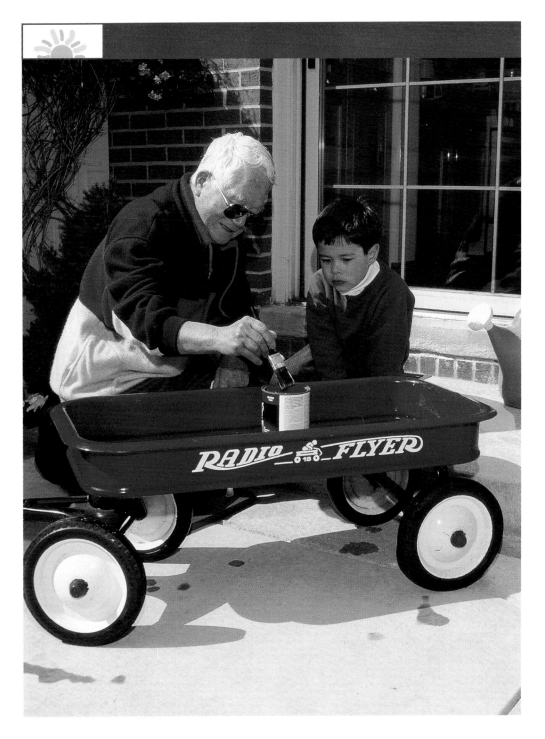

He puts new red paint
on my rusty wagon.

Now I run with my shiny red wagon.

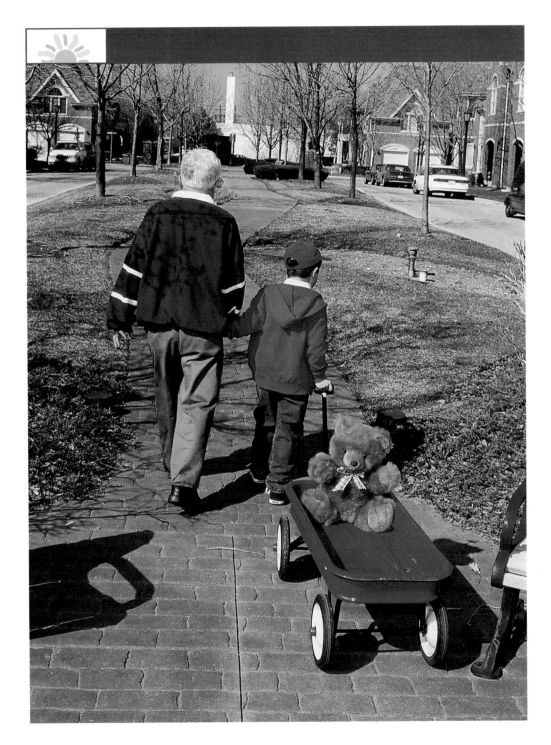

I take my shiny red wagon everywhere with me.

Word List

red	rubs
rest	run
rides	rust
rim	rusty
rocks	

Note to Parents and Educators

The books in the Phonics series of the Wonder Books are based on current research which supports the idea that our brains are pattern detectors rather than rules appliers. This means children learn to read easier when they are taught the familiar spelling patterns found in English. As children encounter more complex words, they have greater success in figuring out these words by using the spelling patterns.

Throughout the 35 books, the texts provide the reader with the opportunity to practice and apply knowledge of the sounds in natural language. The 10 books on the long and short vowels introduce the sounds using familiar onsets and rimes, or spelling patterns, for reinforcement. For example, the word "cat" might be used to present the short "a" sound, with the letter "c" being the onset and "-at" being the rime. This approach provides practice and reinforcement of the short "a" sound, as there are many familiar words made with the "-at" rime.

The 21 consonants and the 4 blends ("ch," "sh," "th," and "wh") use many of these same rimes. The letter(s) before the vowel in a word are considered the onset. Changing the onset allows the consonant books in the series to maintain the practice and reinforcement of the rimes. The repeated use of a word or phrase reinforces the target sound.

The number on the spine of each book facilitates arranging the books in the order that children acquire each sound. The books can also be arranged into groups of long vowels, short vowels, consonants, and blends. All the books in each grouping have their numbers printed in the same color on the spine. The books can be grouped and regrouped easily and quickly, depending on the teacher's needs.

The stories and accompanying photographs in this series are based on time-honored concepts in children's literature: Well-written, engaging texts and colorful, high-quality photographs combine to produce books that children want to read again and again.

Dr. Peg Ballard
Minnesota State University, Mankato

Photo Credits

All photos © copyright: Romie Flanagan/Flanagan Publishing Services.
Cover: Romie Flanagan/Flanagan Publishing Services.

Special thanks to the Sanks family

Photo Research: Alice Flanagan
Design and production: Herman Adler Design Group

Library of Congress Cataloging-in-Publication Data

Klingel, Cynthia Fitterer.
    Rusty red : the sound of "r" / by Cynthia Klingel and Robert B. Noyed.
       p. cm. — (Wonder books)
    Summary : Simple text and repetition of the letter "r" help readers
learn how to use this sound.
    ISBN 1-56766-703-1 (lib. bdg. : alk. paper)
    [1. Wagons Fiction. 2. Alphabet.] I. Noyed, Robert B. II. Title.
    III. Series: Wonder books (Chanhassen, Minn.)
PZ7.K6798Ru   1999
[E]—dc21   99-20954
                                                              CIP